Adapted by Elizabeth Phillips
Illustrated by Lori Tyminski
Designed by Tony Fejeran of Disney Publishing's Global Design Group

 A Golden Book • New York

Copyright © 2005 Disney Enterprises, Inc.
All rights reserved under International and Pan-American Copyright Conventions. Published in the United States
by Golden Books, an imprint of Random House Children's Books, a division of Random House, Inc., New York,
and simultaneously in Canada by Random House of Canada Limited, Toronto, in conjunction with Disney Enterprises, Inc.
Golden Books, A Golden Book, A Little Golden Book, the G colophon,
and the distinctive gold spine are registered trademarks of Random House, Inc.
Library of Congress Control Number: 2005920989
ISBN: 0-7364-2333-8
www.goldenbooks.com
www.randomhouse.com/kids/disney
Printed in the United States of America

10 9 8

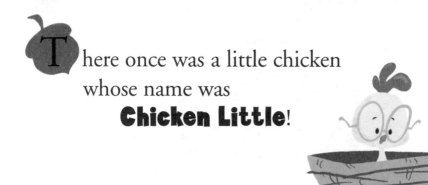

There once was a little chicken whose name was **Chicken Little**!

One day, something fell on Chicken Little's head. He thought the sky was falling!

BONK!

But his dad said it was really just an acorn.

Everyone laughed at Chicken Little—except for his friends,

Abby, **Runt**, and **Fish**.

His father, Buck, didn't laugh, either. But Chicken Little knew that he was ashamed.

Still, Chicken Little held his head high . . .

even when
the other kids
made fun of him . . .

and **even when**
he lost his pants.

You see, all Chicken Little really wanted was to make his father proud. So Chicken Little thought and thought. Then he came up with an idea. He would join the baseball team! Baseball was his dad's favorite sport.

When it came time to play in a real game, everyone thought Chicken Little would strike out.

Instead, he hit a **HOME RUN**!

Buck was very proud of his son, and Chicken Little was very happy.

Father and son would no longer have to hear embarrassing stories about acorns. But then the sky fell. Again! And this time it clearly wasn't an acorn.

BONK!

Chicken Little thought his father would be upset if he told him that the sky had fallen. Again! So Chicken Little called his friends.

Abby and Runt tried to help him figure out what to do. Meanwhile, Fish played with the piece of sky—until . . .

it **flew** away with him!

he went!

Up, **up,** **up**

How would Chicken Little,
Abby, and Runt save Fish?

The three friends found Fish at last. He was in a spaceship! When they saw the aliens leave the spaceship, Chicken Little, Abby, and Runt bravely went inside and rescued their friend.

It was **creepy**!

When they left, nobody noticed a mysterious creature following Chicken Little.

Just then, the aliens returned. They chased
Chicken Little, Abby, Runt, and Fish . . .

out of the spaceship . . .

down
the hill . . .

and **into**
the fields.

The friends had to get to the school to warn
everyone that . . .

**aliens were
attacking!**

CLANG!

CLANG!

CLANG!

But when the townsfolk arrived, the aliens had flown away. No one believed Chicken Little—not even his father.

Chicken Little was very sad. But something strange happened the next day. The mysterious creature arrived at Chicken Little's house!

He was just a cute little alien child who was very unhappy! He wanted Chicken Little to help him get home to his parents.

Chicken Little told his dad about the little alien.
Chicken Little's father finally believed him!
But there was a problem. The aliens
were attacking the town.

And nobody in town knew that the aliens were just looking for their son. It was up to Chicken Little to save the day!

Chicken Little and his dad tried to give the baby back to the aliens. But they were transported into the spaceship instead!

When the aliens found out that their son was
safe, they thanked Chicken Little.

Chicken Little's father was **proud**.

The little chicken was a **big** hero!

And everyone lived
happily ever after.